Dream Bigger

Eric, Be Bold, Be Brave, Be Brilliant

W. F. Duncan

Published in London, England by Peaches Publications, 2021.

www.peachespublications.co.uk

British Library Cataloguing in Publication Data: A catalogue record for this book is available from the British Library.

ISBN: 9781838147280.

Book cover design: Peaches Publications.

Editor: Winsome Duncan and Ms L Duncan.

Typesetter: Winsome Duncan.

Proofreader: Linda Green.

Published by

This book belongs to:

_____

Always Remember to Dream Bigger!

Dedication

This book is dedicated to every little boy who dares to dream the biggest dream he can ever imagine.

#dreambigger

Mummy tells me repeatedly, that I am a handsome boy with a kind heart.

Daddy constantly reminds me that I am
super smart.

Both of my parents tell me daily "Eric dream **BIG**!

And then......

Dream **BIGGER!**'.

Okay, so here goes…

I am changing into a dreaming illuminating figure.

I dream, that I am the first Doctor to find a cure for cancer.

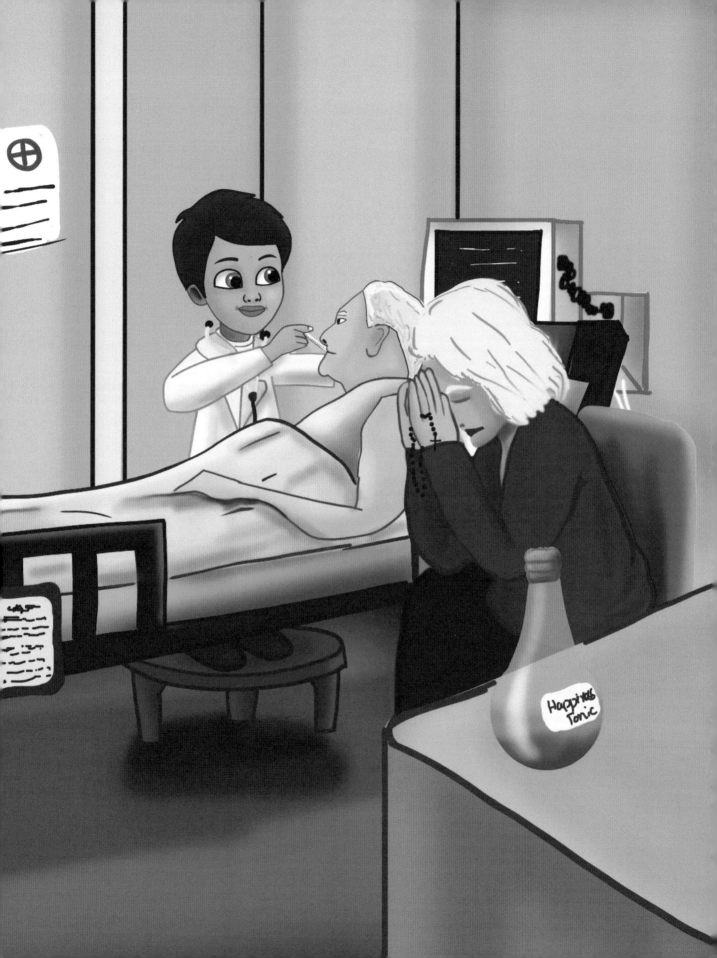

I dream, that I am the first Humanitarian to stop world hunger.

I dream, I am a Philanthropist that shares my wealth to end global poverty.

I dream big, bold and bright dreams.
Come here and dream bigger with me.

I dream, of clean unpolluted air filling up my lungs whilst playing with my friends and having fun.

I dream, of being the first child Astronaut to land on the moon in my private rocket.

I dream, that I am a pioneering Scientist who creates and manufactures the world's first Happiness Tonic.

Today I am dreaming of a loving, and caring family,

Oh wait!

This is my reality!

Lucky dreaming ME.

PLEASE REMEMBER TO GIVE US A REVIEW:

https://amzn.to/3r8iLDu

THANK YOU

A Fun Colouring Book Click Here:

https://amzn.to/2Tfnffg

About The Author

Winsome Duncan is one woman with a HUGE vision of getting her wider community writing books. She has more than 15 years of experience in the book publishing industry. As an author of 16 books, which includes her debut children's book and Amazon number 1 smash hit 'The Popcorn House'. She had committed herself to a #100childrensbooks to diversify children's literature in the UK.

Winsome works tirelessly with budding Authors and Entrepreneurs to help them realise their book-writing dreams. She is the CEO of publishing house called Peaches Publications and not-for-profit social enterprise the Look Like Me Book Challenge® CIC. Which has a particular focus on stories and voices from the Black community which include children age 7 – 18 years old.

Her latest project is a ground-breaking campaign called 'Look Like Me Book Challenge' which supports 30 Black, Asian and Minority Ethnic (BAME) children's authors to write one collective community book. Since the Guardian newspaper published that a mere 5% of BAME main characters are in children's books within the UK. This is compared to 33.5% of BAME school children in education. Inanimate objects are more likely to feature in children's books than Black or Brown faces.

Winsome is passionate about changing this narrative and began a Go Fund Me fund-raising on her birthday weekend of October 2019 for £50,000 to help raise awareness and educate others about the importance of having equal visual representation for multicultural children from diverse heritage.

www.bookconfidencecoach.com and www.peachespublications.co.uk

Printed in Great Britain
by Amazon